MONSTER HUNTERS
hunt for sewer gators

by Jan Fields
Illustrated by Scott Brundage

Calico

An Imprint of Magic Wagon
www.abdopublishing.com

www.abdopublishing.com

Published by Magic Wagon, a division of ABDO, PO Box 398166, Minneapolis, Minnesota 55439. Copyright © 2015 by Abdo Consulting Group, Inc. International copyrights reserved in all countries. No part of this book may be reproduced in any form without written permission from the publisher. Calico™ is a trademark and logo of Magic Wagon.

Printed in the United States of America, North Mankato, Minnesota.
052014
092014

Written by Jan Fields
Illustrated by Scott Brundage
Edited by Tamara L. Britton and Bridget O'Brien
Cover and interior design by Candice Keimig

Library of Congress Cataloging-in-Publication Data

Fields, Jan, author.
 Hunt for sewer gators / by Jan Fields ; illustrated by Scott Brundage.
    pages cm. -- (Monster hunters)
 Summary: Looking for alligators in the sewers of New York City seems like a silly idea to Gabe Brown, but his brother is the creator of internet series, Discover Cryptids, so the filming crew sets out to explore the storm sewers-- but when one of them panics, they get separated and lost.
 ISBN 978-1-62402-045-2
1. Curiosities and wonders--Juvenile fiction. 2. Video recording--Juvenile fiction. 3. Action photography--Juvenile fiction. 4. Storm sewers--Juvenile fiction. 5. Adventure stories. 6. New York (N.Y.)--Juvenile fiction. [1. Curiosities and wonders--Fiction. 2. Sewerage--Fiction. 3. Video recording--Fiction. 4. Adventure and adventurers--Fiction. 5. New York (N.Y.)--Fiction.]
I. Brundage, Scott, illustrator. II. Title.
 PZ7.F479177Hu 2015
 813.6--dc23
                                        2014005821

TABLE of CONTENTS

chapter 1

MONSTER HUNTING

Thirty years had passed since Mount Saint Helens erupted. All around them, Gabe, Tyler and Sean saw signs of both the destruction from the volcano and the return of life to the mountain. Tall dead trees rose up straight into the sky between the younger healthy trees. The area was alive again, but definitely not the same as before.

"Do you have any theories about how the Batsquatch survived the eruption?" Gabe asked his friend Sean. Sean generally knew all the theories and the facts about any cryptid they hunted.

Gabe's best friend, Tyler, spoke up, "It doesn't seem that hard to figure out. It can fly. It flew away." As he talked, he waved his hands and smacked Gabe with his open umbrella. Gabe just shoved it out of the way.

"Birds fly too," Sean said. "Yet many died in the eruption. They couldn't fly fast enough or far enough to escape the poisonous gases and falling ash. However, the Batsquatch may have sensed the impending eruption and fled early." Sean sighed. "You know, there is no logical reason to call this creature a Batsquatch. It doesn't seem to be related to the Sasquatch at all."

"Well, some people believe it has a monkey face," Gabe said.

"And pterodactyl wings," Sean said. "I would have named it Pterobat."

"I think we're losing focus," Tyler said. "We're out here near a dangerous volcano looking for a giant monkey-faced bat that is also psychic."

When Gabe and Sean gave him puzzled looks, Tyler said, "He predicted the volcano in time to fly away."

"I'm not sure that represents any kind of psychic ability," Sean said. "Many animals behave oddly before storms or seismic activity."

"They just might be smarter than people," Tyler said.

Sean shrugged, "Or more sensitive."

"Terrific. Well, let's go find Mr. Sensitive." Tyler marched ahead, smacking Gabe with his open umbrella again as he passed.

"Ouch! Would you put that thing down?" Gabe said. "It's not raining. It's not even cloudy."

"True, but if a giant bat thing flies over, it's not going to grab me. And it's not going to drop anything on me." Tyler tapped the umbrella's camouflage patterned fabric. "I'm practically invisible. You know I hate the flying cryptids. This time I came prepared."

Gabe turned and glared at Sean. "I blame you. The umbrellas were your idea."

Sean shrugged. "After spending three days

in a downpour in Wisconsin tracking the Beast of Bray Road, I try to be ready for anything. If you'll remember, I ended up with a bad cold *and* swimmer's ear from that trip."

"Fine, let's just hurry and get back to camp," Gabe said. "Ben is probably waiting for us."

They picked up their pace, wading through the rough brush. The mountain's new undergrowth wasn't shaded out by mature trees. So they had to watch for branches and roots as they walked. And they couldn't see very far ahead.

Finally, the three broke into a clearing. Gabe sighed with relief. His arms were getting scratched up from all the brush. Then he saw a large black bear shambling along a game trail towards them. The boys froze. The bear froze. The boys and the bear stared at one another without moving.

"What do we do?" Tyler asked, his voice barely a squeak. "Run?"

Sean shook his head. "Black bears run faster than we do. They aren't as aggressive as grizzly bears, but attacks can be fatal."

"You're so cheery," Tyler said.

Gabe looked around. "How about climbing a tree?"

"The bear's too close. You'd never get high enough before it was on us," Sean said.

"You're just a ray of sunshine, you know that?" Tyler said.

"I have an idea," Sean said. "Tyler, hold your umbrella up as high as you can."

Tyler extended his umbrella high into the air. The umbrella wobbled back and forth from Tyler's shaking hands. The bear watched them curiously.

Sean stood beside Tyler and opened his own umbrella, holding it up just below Tyler's. "Stand on Tyler's other side," he told Gabe. "And everyone needs to yell as loud as you can."

Gabe took his place and shouted. "Yah, get

out of here! Go on! Go!" The other boys shouted as well.

The bear shook its head. It took a tentative step toward them.

"Louder!" Sean yelled. "Take a step toward it and shake your umbrella!"

They all took one step forward. Gabe screamed at the top of his lungs. Tyler and Sean shook their umbrellas and bellowed. Gabe figured it was just a matter of minutes before the bear decided to go ahead and kill them for being annoying. Still, he kept yelling.

The bear shook its head again, and then it spun around and ran. The boys cheered. The bear ran faster. Soon it was out of sight. "I can't believe that worked," Tyler said, his voice hoarse from screaming.

"Bears have great noses," Sean said. "But not the best eyesight. So they judge the size of an opponent mostly by the outline. We made a

really big outline and a really big noise. It was completely logical really."

As they were panting with relief, Gabe's stepbrother Ben stepped out of the brush at the side of the clearing. "What's all the yelling about?" he said. "You guys better have seen a Batsquatch, because you probably scared away everything in a half mile area."

"Sorry about that. Things just got *grizzly* here for a minute," Tyler said with a grin. "We couldn't *bear* to be quiet."

Gabe groaned and gave his friend a playful shove. Tyler giggled. Sean just shook his head and muttered, "I told you it wasn't a grizzly."

Tyler ran to tell Ben about the bear. Sean followed slowly, closing his umbrella and putting it away as he walked. Looking around the woods, Gabe wondered if their bear encounter ruined their chances of seeing a Batsquatch.

Then, he spotted something high in one of the half-burned trees. For a second, he wondered if it might be a bear cub clinging to the tree's trunk. Then in a burst of movement, the creature flew over Gabe's head and deeper into the forest.

"Hey, did you see that?" Gabe yelled.

"What?" Ben asked. "Did you scare another bear?"

Gabe shook his head. Exactly what had he seen? An eagle? A buzzard? A Batsquatch? He might never know. He trotted over to the rest of the group with a sigh.

chapter 2

BEING FOLLOWED

Barely two weeks later, the monster hunters were in a place as different from Mount Saint Helens as Gabe could imagine. He stood "on Top of the Rock," on the observation deck at Rockefeller Center in New York City. The guys had spent the morning playing tourist since none of them had ever been there before.

Gabe walked close to the thick glass that separated visitors from a terrifying 69-floor drop. There were viewers to give visitors a closer look, but Gabe found the view amazing enough without them.

His brother walked up behind him and peered through the glass. Gabe cleared his throat. He had a question he'd been wondering ever since

Ben announced this investigation. "Why are we here?"

Ben looked surprised. "Well, this platform isn't as high as the one on the Empire State Building, but I liked the idea of the glass panels."

"No. I meant why are we in New York City?"

"You know why. We're investigating alligators in the city's sewers."

Gabe rolled his eyes. "But that's just goofy. You know there aren't *really* any alligators in the sewers here. Usually you pick subjects that make *some* sense."

"I'm surprised at you," Ben said. "Where's your open mind?"

"It was open for ape men and flying things and the chupacabra," Gabe said. "But alligators in the sewers? In a city this populated? I almost got squashed in a candy store in Times Square today because there are so many people – how could alligators hide anywhere here?"

"Well, they live in the sewers," Ben said. "There aren't a lot of tourists in the sewers. Besides, we've not yet begun. Wait until we meet with Hanson McCall and hear what he has to say. He believes they're here."

Hanson McCall was an author. He'd written a bunch of books on different urban legends. He was working on one that featured the alligator sewer story. They had an appointment to meet him after supper.

Gabe wasn't sure why he wasn't more enthusiastic about this investigation. New York City was cool. Maybe he was just ready to go home. The summer of cryptid hunting for Ben's internet show, *Discover Cryptids*, had been great. More than once, it got a little scary, but Gabe wouldn't have missed it for anything. Still, he was feeling homesick.

Gabe's eyes swept over the other tourists on the platform. Then he spotted someone who

looked familiar. The man was thin but wiry with a scruffy beard and long matted hair. He wore several layers of tattered clothes, which seemed hot for the late summer day. Gabe wondered why the man looked so familiar. Then he realized he'd seen the same man that morning in Central Park and then again on the street.

He'd not paid the man a lot of attention. Ben had warned him against making eye contact with strangers in the city, but that seemed a little mean to Gabe. What if, he wondered, someone in their group had made eye contact with the strange man and now he was following them?

Gabe reached out and tugged on his brother's arm, while keeping his eyes on the stranger. Ben slowly turned around, "Yeah?"

Just then, the stranger looked right at Gabe. The man's face turned panicked, and he backed away. Gabe nodded in the stranger's direction. "That man. I think he's following us."

"What man?" Ben asked just as the stranger stepped out of sight between small groups of tourists.

"He's gone now. It was a scruffy guy. He looked homeless," Gabe said. "I saw him in the park this morning and on the street when we got here. I didn't really make the connection until he showed up here on the platform."

Ben shrugged. "Sadly, there are a lot of homeless people in New York City. It's a problem for most big cities. I expect you just saw different guys and they're running together in your memory."

Gabe shook his head. He was sure that wasn't the case.

Tyler trotted up to them. "I can see the Empire State building from the south view. Wouldn't it be cool if King Kong were hanging from the top? Talk about a cryptid!"

Ben laughed. "If you saw King Kong, we'd

definitely skip the investigation of alligators in the sewers." He looked around at the slowly building crowd. "Have you seen Sean? We need to gather up and head to supper so we can make our meeting with Mr. McCall."

"He's back looking at the Empire State Building," Tyler said, pointing. "I think he was doing math problems. He has no idea how to have fun."

"Yes, I do," Sean said, slipping through a group of tourists to join them. "I was estimating the size of King Kong based on what this guidebook says about the Empire State Building. Then I was estimating his weight. I don't believe an ape of that size could climb a building. It probably couldn't even walk."

"That will be very comforting if we ever run into King Kong." Ben began to herd them toward the doors. Gabe turned for one last glance through the thick glass. The late afternoon sun

hitting the glass made a slight mirror effect. Gabe saw a face looking back at him. It wasn't his face. Instead, it was the bearded stranger. He spun around but couldn't spot the man.

Ben tugged on his arm. "Earth to Gabe. Let's go. We still need to decide where to go for supper. I don't want to be late for our meeting."

"Right," Gabe mumbled as he stumbled along beside his brother. "Sorry." As they walked to the elevator, Gabe wondered if he was seeing things. Maybe it really was time to be done with the monster hunting.

chapter 3
EARLY EVIDENCE

They squeezed into a cab for the drive to Brooklyn. There, they had some fantastic pizza. Tyler ate so much that he waddled when they left the place. Ben decided it would do them all good to walk to Hanson McCall's apartment. "It'll give our food a chance to digest," he said.

"We would have to walk to China for Tyler's food to digest," Gabe said.

They all laughed, though Tyler groaned afterwards. "Don't make me laugh."

"You really should learn portion control," Sean suggested.

"He did control his portions," Gabe said with a laugh. "He made sure he got a big portion of each of the pizzas."

By the time they arrived at McCall's building, Tyler had stopped moaning with each step. The author had a tiny apartment in the old building. The walls of the room that served as both living room and bedroom were lined with bookcases. Every shelf was crammed with books, magazines and stacks of papers.

"You're quite a reader," Ben said, looking around.

"Researcher," Hanson corrected, pushing a pair of glasses up on his nose. He was a small man with a tendency to stoop. Thick red hair stood up all over his head. "I dig into secrets no one wants to talk about. In many ways, we have a lot in common, but you use a camera to show people what you've discovered. I use books." He scooped up armloads of papers from a lumpy couch and gestured for them to sit. Ben, Gabe and Tyler sat. Sean stood next to one of the bookcases and stared at the shelves in fascination.

Hanson narrowed his eyes at Sean for a moment, then simply said, "Look, but don't touch. I have a system."

Gabe wondered what kind of system could produce so much mess. Ben asked for permission to tape the interview. Hanson quickly agreed.

Gabe stood and took a spot where he could film the man speaking. Hanson sat down in a folding chair facing the couch. "So, you're interested in the alligators in the sewer?"

"We're interested in exploring the possibility," Ben said. "Though I understand there are a number of arguments against the existence of reptiles in the sewer."

Hanson shook his head and ran a hand through his wild hair. "I've heard all the arguments. No one could flush an alligator that is big enough to survive the trip. The water is too cold. There isn't enough food." He ticked each argument off on his fingers.

"But you don't consider those valid?" Ben asked.

"Every year sewer workers find scores of turtles and fish in the sewers. The city is proud of the workers' efforts to rehabilitate the animals and release them back into the wild. But that also means reptiles can live in the sewers since turtles are reptiles. And it means there are food sources." The man hopped up and began to pace around the small room. "Plus, there are warm water animals surviving in cold water lakes and streams all over the world."

"We discovered that when we explored Lake Tahoe," Sean said. "The populations of largemouth bass are a problem for the lake, even though they shouldn't be able to survive the winter cold there."

Hanson nodded. "Plus, we flatly know alligators have been found all over New York." He rushed to a pile of albums near one of

the bookshelves and picked up the biggest scrapbook. He showed them cuttings and news stories of alligators in New York.

"So you think someone is flushing these guys?" Tyler asked.

Hanson shook his head. "No, that is ridiculous. But, there are plenty of storm drains that could easily fit a young alligator. If you wanted to dispose of your kid's growing alligator, you could just walk outside and toss it in the storm drain."

"None of these are giant alligators," Ben said, pointing at a photo of an 18-inch alligator on the hood of a police car. "The legend is specifically about giant mutated alligators."

"I do have one account of a six-foot long alligator from the *New York Times*," Hanson said. "It happened in February of 1935. Some boys were shoveling snow into a manhole when an alligator tried to climb out. They apparently

lassoed the creature and dragged it to the street. Then they killed it with shovels."

"Wow," Tyler said. "Too bad there's not a picture of that!"

"The thirties were really the most popular time for alligator sightings," Hanson said. "Some people speculate that there must have been a thriving exotic pet trade in alligators at the time."

"Still, even six-foot is within the limits of an ordinary alligator," Ben said. "Not a mutant."

"I'll admit, I haven't seen any evidence of giant alligators," Hanson said. "Or mutated albino alligators. But the arguments against any alligators surviving in the sewers of New York simply aren't valid. All kinds of things survive in the sewers of New York."

"Have you been down in the sewers?" Ben asked.

Hanson glanced at the camera in Gabe's hands. "That would be illegal wouldn't it? You'd

have to get permission, and no one's giving out permission to hunt for gators in the sewers. That is one story that the city is very tired of."

Ben waved for Gabe to stop filming. Gabe lowered the camera, and Hanson immediately looked more relaxed. "So, do you know anyone who has been down in the sewers and might talk about it on tape?"

Hanson nodded. "There are urban explorers all over New York. Some go into abandoned buildings. Some poke around in some of the off-limits areas of the subway. And some go down into the sewers. All of those activities are illegal."

"And if I needed to speak to one of them?" Ben said.

"Well, if I had broken the law and entered the sewers, I would probably have gone with Max Payne. He's taken people down to film before. And he has tons of photos of the sewer online. Clearly he doesn't mind being quite public about

his activities. You can find his contact information online."

Ben had Gabe shoot some footage of Hanson's alligator scrapbook and all of his bookcases. He also took some still shots of the man bent over his battered desk, peering at a photo with a magnifying glass. Then Ben thanked Hanson, and they left.

When they reached the street, Ben asked Gabe to shoot a little footage up and down the street. "We can use it as filler if we need it," Ben said.

Gabe nodded and lifted the camera to pan the street. The group walked along slowly as Gabe filmed.

Tyler looked back at the apartment where Hanson lived. "That man was a flake."

"That seems unfair," Sean said. "Mr. McCall has clearly done a lot of research. I think that's important to remember. He isn't just making these things up."

Tyler grunted. "Right, he's just talking to people who make things up."

"No one made up photographic evidence," Sean said.

Ben cleared his throat. "Enough arguing. Hanson certainly was helpful. When we get back to the hotel, Sean can track down this Max Payne so we can set up an appointment."

"Are we going down in the sewers with him?" Tyler asked eagerly.

"If so, I believe I'll pass," Sean said. "I have no interest in the kinds of bacteria and vermin that inhabit sewer systems."

"Don't worry about it," Ben said. "We're not going into the sewers. As Hanson pointed out, it's illegal. I tried going through all the proper channels, but apparently they're very tired of the alligator story. And our little internet show doesn't have enough viewers to impress them."

Gabe turned around to film behind them.

His attention was drawn to a quick movement on the other side of the street. He swung the camera towards it and saw a surprised face right in his viewscreen. It was the same bearded man from the observation platform. "Ben," Gabe yelped. "There he is again."

Ben turned around as the man dashed into an alley between two tall apartment buildings. "Who?"

"The homeless guy from the observation platform," Gabe said. "He just ran into that alley."

His brother frowned. "That's not really very likely."

Gabe turned the camera's viewscreen toward his brother and ran the video back. Then he froze on the man's face. "That's him!"

"I don't know, Gabe," Ben said. "He looks like a lot of guys we've passed today."

Sean stepped up and peered over Ben's shoulder. "Do you have a shot that shows his

clothes? It would probably be easier to identify specific clothing."

Gabe ran through the video but the full figure shots of the man were too brief because the man ran into the alley, and he was partially obscured by cars.

"If it's not the same man, why did he run?" Gabe asked.

"Sometimes homeless people are in some trouble with the law," Ben said. "He may simply have been freaked out by the camera. He just doesn't want his photo taken."

Gabe sighed. He was disappointed that Ben didn't take this more seriously. The guy was clearly following them, and they needed to find out why.

chapter 4
A SECRET ADMIRER

It didn't take long to track down Max Payne. He had a big, flashy website where he claimed to have investigated secret places all over the world. The site had a huge gallery of photos, so Gabe figured he really had been everywhere. Still, to him, the tone of the site sounded a lot like bragging.

"We could email the guy," Sean said. "His email address is right here."

"So is his phone number. I think I'll just call," Ben said. Sean wrinkled his nose and Ben laughed. "I know. I'm an old fashioned guy." Ben walked off to the far corner of the room so he could concentrate on the call.

"I'm not going into any sewer," Sean said. "I'll just stay here and offer remote support."

"When have we ever needed remote support?" Tyler asked.

Sean turned and looked at him. "It's something new."

Tyler flopped down on the bed beside the desk. "Well, I'm looking forward to exploring. Just think. It's some place where almost no one has ever been!"

"I wouldn't get my hopes up," Gabe said. "Ben will never go along with doing something that's against the law. And he doubly wouldn't let us do it." Gabe leaned against the edge of the desk. He wished Ben would let them go. What if they actually found an alligator? Even a turtle would be pretty cool.

Sean just shook his head and turned back to the computer. "Good. I have no interest in wading in poop."

"Okay, guys, we have an interview," Ben said as he walked across the room to them. "But it'll

have to be very early tomorrow morning. Let's pack up what we need so we're good to go first thing."

Tyler groaned. "How early are we talking about?"

"Seven," Ben said. "That works well for me anyway. I have an appointment to talk to a sewer worker in the morning. I should be able to get both in before lunch."

"Well, in that case, I'm ready for bed." Tyler threw himself on the nearest bed and began fake snoring. It was only slightly quieter than his real snoring.

Ben smacked Tyler's sneaker. "Turning in is a good idea. We've had a big day. Since we only have the one bathroom, we'll take turns. I'm first." He strode across the room and into the bathroom.

"Hey, how is that fair?" Gabe asked.

Ben poked his head out the door. "I'm oldest."

After a day rushing all over New York City,

they all slept hard. Even Tyler's snoring couldn't keep Gabe awake. Still, it made an impression on some level because Gabe dreamed he was running through the sewer, chased by something huge that wheezed and rattled in the darkness.

In the dream, Gabe was alone in the dark with the wheezing monster. Gabe didn't dare to turn and look at it. He focused on running. The sewer was full of thick, deep mud. He ran in slow motion, desperate to get away. The wheezing breath began to blow right on his neck, hot and slightly stinky.

That hot breath pulled Gabe out of the dream. He discovered Tyler had rolled over in the big double bed they had to share and was snoring almost directly in Gabe's ear. "Yuck," Gabe complained, giving his friend a shove. "Go snore on your side."

Tyler woke enough to grumble and roll over. Gabe lay back down, but found he had trouble falling back to sleep. He finally climbed out of bed and shuffled off to the bathroom for a drink of water.

He carried the glass back into the big room and peered out the window at the New York City night. Could there be alligators in the sewers underneath him? He shrugged. Even if there were, they probably didn't snore. With a sigh, he climbed back in bed.

The alarm clock woke them far too early the next morning. There was a general air of grumbling and snappy tempers as they got

ready to go. "I hope we're eating before we go anywhere," Tyler said.

"We'll get breakfast right after we meet with Max Payne," Ben promised. "I didn't want to get up any earlier so we'll just have to wait."

Tyler groaned. "Just don't leave me on the street if I faint from hunger."

Finally they were all dressed and ready. They scrambled to grab cameras, a hand-held light, and a recorder. Then they hustled out to catch a cab. They'd barely reached the street when Gabe stumbled to a stop. A man was hurrying toward them. It was the same homeless guy Gabe had seen the day before.

"Mr. Green?" the man asked quietly.

Ben turned toward the man. He hesitated only a moment before smiling and saying, "That's me. Can I help you?"

The man stopped slightly out of hand-shaking reach. He pulled a battered hat off his head and

twisted it in his hands. "I just wanted to tell you that I'm a big fan of *Discover Cryptids*. When I saw you were coming to New York, I knew I wanted to meet you."

"I'm pleased to meet a fan," Ben said. "So, you haven't seen any alligators in New York have you?"

The man shook his head. "I've been in the sewers, and I've seen some weird stuff, but no alligators."

"Weird stuff?" Tyler echoed.

"Not cryptid weird," the man said. "Just New Yorkers weird. I've seen some big eels, for instance. I've even eaten a couple."

"Ewww," Tyler said and Gabe poked him in the arm, but the man just smiled.

"I'd be willing to bet you have some great stories," Ben said. "And I wish we had time to hear them, but we have an appointment right now. We're going to have to run, but I'm really glad to meet you."

"And I'm glad that Ben has to admit you're real!" Gabe said.

The man looked at Gabe sheepishly. "Sorry. I didn't mean to freak you out. It just took a while to work up my courage to talk to your brother. Most folks would rather not talk to homeless people."

"Well, I'm glad you talked to us. And I do hope we run into you again while we're here," Ben said. "But we *really* have to run now."

"Right, sorry. Good luck with your 'gator hunt," the man said.

Ben stepped out closer to the street and waved down a cab. "Thanks," he said to the homeless man, then he ushered the boys into the cab.

The man waved as they pulled out into the street. Gabe sat back in the cab and crossed his arms. It felt good to show Ben that he wasn't imagining things. Then he thought of something weird. "How do you think that guy kept finding us in the city?"

Ben shrugged. "The first time was probably a coincidence. You first saw him in Central Park, right? He might spend time there regularly, I suppose."

"Then what?" Gabe asked.

"Then he followed us," Sean said.

"Which is just creepy," Tyler added.

"Maybe a little," Ben agreed. "But *Discover Cryptids* doesn't have enough fans to be picky. I guess I can understand him being a little nervous. Most people try not to see the homeless."

Gabe felt a mix of emotions. He was kind of sorry for the stranger and a little bit creeped out. It must be terrible to be afraid to talk to anyone because you're not sure how they'll react. Plus, he couldn't even imagine not having a home to go to at night. Even with all their travelling for the show, they also had a home waiting when the summer was over.

KENNEDY

chapter 5

FALSE ALARM

The drive to Queens took a while, so Gabe sat back and gazed out the window. Soon the passing buildings began to blur, and he nodded off. He woke to someone poking him in the shoulder. "We're here!" Tyler half-shouted in his ear. "Let's get going. Breakfast is waiting for me somewhere."

"Ouch. You didn't have to yell," Gabe complained. "I wasn't sleeping *that* soundly."

"I don't know why you were sleeping at all," Tyler said. "We just slept."

"Some of us slept better than others," Gabe said. "Mister Snores-a-lot."

Tyler raised his eyebrows. "I do not snore."

Gabe, Sean and Ben spoke at once. "Yes, you do."

Finally, Gabe half stumbled out of the car and looked up at another tall apartment building. People who lived in New York must feel like someone's looking down on them all the time. Tyler tugged on his arm, muttering, "Breakfast." Gabe hurried up the apartment steps to join Ben and Sean at the door.

Max Payne buzzed them in right away, and they took the elevator up to his floor. Max turned out to be younger than he looked on the website. Gabe doubted he was much older than Ben. His thinning hair had looked grey in the photos but was really pale blonde, and his face was full of enthusiasm for his topic.

"New York City has a lot of exciting choices for underground exploration," he said. "My favorites are the subway tunnels, which are home to all sorts of things – human and animal."

"We're mostly focusing this show on the possibility of alligators in the sewers," Ben said.

"There's plenty of sewer tunnels to hide in," Max said. "Miles and miles."

"There are actually over 6,000 miles of sewer pipes," Sean said. "With over 135,000 sewer catch basins."

Max looked at Sean in surprise. Sean shrugged. "I like to be accurate."

"Well, good for you! I haven't been in all 6,000 miles of pipes, of course."

"That would be impossible," Sean said. "The smallest sewer pipes would barely fit your arm. They feed into progressively larger pipes and eventually tunnels."

"Right," Max said, frowning slightly at Sean. "Those are the tunnels where I've been. Some of them are big enough to drive a golf cart into. They're plenty big enough to fit an alligator. You know, the sewer alligator story isn't just some urban legend though. There have been articles in the *New York Times*. And a sewer expert was

42

quoted for a book. He said there were whole nests of alligators down there."

Sean leaned forward, clearly gearing up to share what he'd learned, but Ben put his hand on Sean's arm. "Have you personally seen any alligators?" Ben asked.

Max shook his head. "But to be fair, I've spent a lot more time in the subway than the sewers. I wouldn't be surprised to run across an alligator some day. So, you're looking for a guide into the sewers?"

Ben shook his head. "It's illegal, and I don't think it's the place for kids, either. Though if you have some footage or even photos that you can share with us, that would be great."

Max grinned. "Well, you definitely don't want to get caught. And there are dangers. In some places, there are pockets of hydrogen sulfide gas. People can't breathe that and it's killed workers in the past. But I know my way around. We'd be

safe enough. And what better time is there for having adventures than when you're a kid?"

"And what better way to ensure these guys' parents never let them work with me again?" Ben asked mildly.

Max held up his hands. "Okay. It's your call. Come on, I'll show you some of the footage I have. I cued it up on my computer just in case you wanted to see it. I'd let you use any of it, but you'll need to credit me in the show."

"Of course," Ben said.

Max began playing the footage. Ben and Sean bent over to stare fixedly at the monitor. Max pulled Gabe away from the others and whispered, "I just wanted to tell you that if *any* of you change your minds. I'd be glad to show you the sewers." He pressed a business card into Gabe's hand.

Gabe glanced over at the computer and sighed. "My brother won't change his mind," he said softly.

Max shrugged. "So don't bring him along."

Gabe looked at the man in shock. Was this adult suggesting he sneak around behind his brother's back? What kind of guy does that? "I'll think about it," he said.

"You do that." Max gave Gabe a friendly clap on the back and walked back over to the rest of the group. They only spent a few more minutes at the apartment. Tyler resorted to grabbing his stomach and moaning to move them along.

"I'd better feed my staff," Ben said. "I might need them later. Thanks for everything."

"No problem," Max said. "And remember, I'm here if you want a tour of the sewer. I can't promise alligators, but I can promise the trip would be unforgettable."

"I don't think so," Ben said. He herded the guys out of the apartment. "So where should we go for breakfast?"

"Some place close," Tyler said.

Sean held up his smartphone and stared at the screen. "There's a diner in walking distance and a grocery that says it's also a deli."

"Diner," Tyler gasped. "Eggs, bacon, toast. It's my only hope."

Ben shook his head but said, "Diner it is. Sean, you can be our navigator."

Up ahead, a small crowd of people practically blocked the sidewalk. They walked up and tried to peek at what was inside the knot of people. Gabe ducked down low and slipped between two adults.

He reached the center of the group and he pushed a woman's flapping raincoat out of his face and found himself nose to snout with a gigantic alligator crawling out of a sewer manhole. Gabe shrieked, scrambling backwards as quickly as he could. To his surprise, the adults around him just laughed.

One man reached down and helped Gabe to

his feet. "It's not real," he said. "It's a promotion for some movie. They just finished setting it up a little while ago."

Gabe looked closely at the alligator. It looked amazingly real, though it wasn't moving of course. Gabe took a step closer and touched the alligator. It was hard and rough.

"Gabe!" Ben's voice cut through the crowd and Gabe began to squeeze back through the people. He finally popped out back beside his brother.

"Did I hear you shriek?" Tyler asked with a grin.

"You should see that thing up close," Gabe said. "It really looks real."

Sean pointed at a poster stuck to the wall next to the crowd. "I assume it's promoting that movie." The poster showed an alligator and a shark fighting in the middle of the street. Across the top, it read, "The Big Apple Gets Bitten."

"Sharks vs. Alligators?" Tyler said. "That would be cool."

"How exactly are sharks supposed to get on the streets of New York?" Sean asked. "The entire premise is silly."

"But cool," Tyler insisted.

The crowd was finally growing bored with looking at the alligator, and they began to thin out. Two men walked up carrying sawhorses with "Shark vs. Gator" stenciled on them. "Excuse us," one of the men called. "Coming through."

The crowd broke up and the men set the sawhorses on either side of the alligator. Sean watched them with crossed arms. "That's not even a real manhole cover."

"Of course not, kid," one of the men said. "We couldn't clog up a real manhole cover." Then he grinned. "Looks right scary though, don't you think?"

"Yeah," Gabe agreed and Tyler snickered behind him.

"So are we going to see sharks coming out of the sewers too?" Tyler asked.

The man laughed. "You never know."

chapter 6

Into the
Sewer

Tyler finally managed to haul them away from the movie display. The diner was just around the corner. It reminded Gabe of one he had seen in a picture hanging in the art room of his school back home. His art teacher said it was a famous painting by someone named Hopper. Gabe remembered the name because it sounded funny. He wondered if the painter got teased for it when he was a kid.

Tyler ordered enough food for two kids. Gabe knew he'd get full before he ate half of it. Actually he might manage a little more than half. Tyler was a big eater. Gabe ordered a couple of pancakes. They weren't as good as the ones his mom made, but they weren't too bad either.

Ben gobbled down his own order of toast and bacon, and then glanced at his watch with a yelp. "I'm going to be late if I don't dash right now. Can you guys get back to the hotel okay?"

"Sure," Gabe said. "We can take the subway."

"Great. We'll do something cool this afternoon. I promise." Ben walked to the counter and paid their bill, then waved at the guys before heading out of the diner.

"You know," Tyler said as he stretched out his legs and patted his full stomach. "Now that I'm not starving, it sounds kind of dull to hang out in the room."

"Not to me," Sean said. "I'm looking forward to editing some of the video we've shot so far."

"Yeah, you're a thrill-seeker," Tyler said. "Still, I wish Ben had let that Max guy take us into the sewer."

Gabe sat forward in his seat. "You won't believe what that guy said to me. He actually

suggested we sneak out and let him take us into the sewer behind Ben's back."

Tyler perked up. "Really? Do you think he'd take us this morning?"

"No!" Gabe said. "Actually, probably yes, but we're not going. Ben would freak."

Tyler shrugged. "Maybe not. Especially if we brought back some cool footage of an alligator in the sewer. Even a fish or a turtle would be great for the show."

Gabe shook his head. "Ben would be mad."

"This is our last investigation for the summer," Tyler said. "Ben can't take us with him once school starts anyway. By next summer he'll cool down. And isn't that what an investigation is all about, actually investigating?"

"Well, I'm not going," Sean said. "Sewers are filled with bacteria and dangerous gases. Plus, they're just disgusting. I'd much rather work on the editing."

"I'm going," Tyler insisted. "You can stay behind with Mr. Thrillseeker if you want, Gabe. But if this guy is willing to take me, I'm going."

Gabe frowned. He didn't like the idea of Tyler going into the sewer alone with Max. What if something happened? He also knew that it was impossible to talk Tyler out of something when he was worked up. Tyler was his best friend. He couldn't just leave him to do something that dangerous, could he?

"Okay," Gabe said. "We'll call him, and I'll go with you." Tyler smirked in triumph. "But if Max can't go right now, we shelve this idea. And once we're there, I decide what we do. No getting crazy."

"Fine, fine," Tyler said. "Just call."

Gabe pulled the half-crumpled business card out of his jeans and punched in the number on his cell phone. As he listened to it ring, he hoped the man wouldn't answer. Naturally, he couldn't be that lucky.

"Hello, Max Payne!"

"Um, Mr. Payne? This is Gabe Brown. We met this morning."

"Right! Does this mean you've changed your mind? Great!"

"Well, yeah," Gabe said. Now his only hope was that they couldn't go right away. "I was wondering if you could take Tyler and me into the sewers this morning. Like right away."

"Sure," Max said. "I know exactly where to take you in. You'll love it. There's a storm drain that actually dumps right out into the Atlantic Ocean. If you can come right away, we should get there right at low tide. It's easiest to explore then."

"Okay, we'll get a cab to your place right now," Gabe said and Tyler whooped beside him. His pancakes suddenly felt too heavy in his stomach as it clenched in panic. What had he just agreed to?

The three guys headed out of the diner and Sean said, "So, what am I supposed to do if Ben gets back before you guys? I'm not lying for you."

"No, that's okay. You should just tell him. He's going to find out anyway." The heavy feeling in Gabe's stomach got heavier. This had to be the worst idea in the whole world. "We'll try to be quick. Then we can tell Ben face to face."

"Well, try not to get hurt," Sean said. Then he turned and headed to the subway platform.

Tyler was practically bouncing beside Gabe. "I'll get a cab," he said. He flagged one down and they climbed in. Gabe read the address off the business card, and they were on their way. Gabe's stomach refused to settle down, and he felt distinctly green by the time they reached Max's apartment.

Max Payne was waiting for them on the sidewalk in front of his apartment. "Glad to see you guys. Let's go have an adventure!"

Max flagged another cab, though this time they only went a few miles. "We still have a little walk," he said. "But no point having too much attention when we access the sewer."

To Gabe's surprise, the manhole wasn't in the middle of the street or even the sidewalk. Instead, it was in an empty lot. It looked like it was cut right into the dirt, though when Max lifted the cover, Gabe saw rungs leading down into the ground.

Max pulled some sort of electronic device from his backpack. It was attached to a length of thin rope. He lowered it down the manhole. "I've never found any bad air down this particular hole, because it's really a storm drain under it, but it always pays to be careful. Sewer gases can knock you right out." He hauled the device back up and checked the read out. "Looks like we're good to go. I'll go first. Then you guys, one at a time. We'll leave the cover off since this is pretty

out of the way. With the weeds and all, someone would have to be right on top of us to see that we've gone down."

"Is that safe?" Gabe asked. "Couldn't someone fall in?"

"It should be fine," Max said.

Tyler leaned close to Gabe and whispered fiercely. "Don't be such a worrywart. He'll think we're not cool."

Gabe sighed. Maybe he wasn't cool, but he didn't like any of this. He watched Max climb down into the hole. Tyler followed second. Gabe dragged the heavy manhole so it at least partly covered the hole. That should be somewhat safer. Then he squeezed through the remaining gap and climbed down the rungs.

When he reached the bottom, he looked around, amazed. The tunnel was huge. More than tall enough to stand. It was more rectangular than round, so it looked more like a

long corridor than a pipe. The floor was slightly bowed with high sides and a low middle. That meant a rush of water ran down the middle, but they had a nice wide dry shoulder to walk on.

"Things look different in some of the other sewers," Max said. "The sewer pipe is sometimes completely round and lined with brick. They're still huge though. But the New York sewers were built and added onto for years. So not all of it looks the same."

All in all, it looked a lot cleaner than Gabe expected. Somehow, he'd envisioned some deep pool of murky water that they'd have to half swim through. When he mentioned that, Max laughed. "This is actually part of the storm drain system, so you shouldn't run into actual sewage. Still, you never know what could end up in a storm drain. I certainly wouldn't wash my face in this water."

"Don't worry," Tyler said. "That's one thing I won't be doing."

Max pointed along the tunnel. "In that direction, the water eventually dumps into the ocean. Unfortunately, that means the water rises a little with the tides, so this will have to be a quick trip. Anyway, off we go."

Max passed out helmets with lights on them and rubber boots. Gabe wondered just how much stuff Max had crammed in that backpack. He pulled on the boots even though the edge where they walked was pretty dry. Still, as they walked, he began to appreciate the boots since they passed a few suspicious clumps on the ledge that he wouldn't want on his shoes.

Gabe carried the camera he'd worn since they arrived in New York. He shot footage of everything. If he was going to get into big trouble with Ben, he'd at least have something useful for the show in the end.

As they walked, they passed side pipes that dumped trickles of water into the bigger pipe where they were. "You'll be amazed by this place," Max said. "In most of the city, the sewers run right into the storm drains, but we're heading to a section that is all storm run-off. Otherwise, it couldn't run into the ocean untreated. Anyway, I figured your brother would prefer you guys stayed out of the regular sewers. There's less risk of gases here."

It was hard to keep track of how long they walked. The sound of running water and the endless pipes made it seem much longer than Gabe's watch suggested. Finally, they reached the biggest storm drains. This didn't look like a pipe at all. It looked like a huge room with thick columns holding up a brick ceiling.

They had to wade in water up to mid-shin and Gabe appreciated the rubber boots all over

again. "The water won't get deeper than this, will it?" he asked.

"It will, but we'll be long gone before then," Max told him. "Now this would be the area to find an alligator, or any other creature. There is always water here, though sometimes it's brackish with backup from the ocean.

As they waded, Gabe kept his eyes fixed on the water, looking for signs of life. Suddenly, something long and wiggly swam right by his right leg, bumping him slightly. Gabe yelled as the creature swam toward Tyler.

"Snake!" Tyler screamed, dancing around in the water. The creature swam right between his legs and Tyler shrieked. Then he took off, running hard.

"Tyler, stop!" Gabe yelled. He knew Tyler was terrified of snakes. In his panic, he could get hurt or lost in the sewer.

"Calm down, kid!" Max yelled. "It's just an eel."

Tyler either didn't hear him or didn't believe
him, because he kept running. Gabe had no
choice. He couldn't leave Tyler on his own. He
ran after him.

"Oh, come on," Max yelled. "You two come
back here. This place isn't safe on your own. We
have to get out of here soon."

Gabe believed him. He just didn't think he
had any choice.

chapter 7

Exploring the Sewer

Gabe ran through the storm drain, yelling Tyler's name. He could hear the splashing of Tyler's footsteps, but couldn't see him in the gloom.

They ran back into the narrower tunnel. Gabe didn't have enough breath to yell anymore. He just hoped Tyler wore out soon. They needed to turn back around and find Max. He didn't know how deep the water would get at high tide, so he wanted to be out of the tunnel by then.

Finally, he saw Tyler on the narrow patch of dry tunnel near the right wall. He stood bent nearly double as he worked to catch his breath. Gabe closed the distance between them quickly and grabbed Tyler's arm. For more than a minute,

they both just gasped. Then Gabe managed to speak. "What's wrong with you? You could get lost down here!"

Tyler looked around at the rushing water. "Snakes," he said. "There are snakes in there."

"It wasn't a snake. It was an eel."

Tyler shook his head. "I saw it. It was a snake."

"Not according to Max Payne, and he's the expert. We need to find him and get out of here." He tugged on Tyler's arm. Tyler pulled back. "I'm not going back down there. That thing was a snake!"

"I don't care if it was an alligator," Gabe snapped. "We have to get out of here. Come on." He hauled hard on Tyler's arm, and his friend stumbled along beside him.

The water had gotten deeper and the dry shoulder was too narrow for walking. They had no choice but to wade through the water. Tyler's head jerked back and forth as he tried to

64

watch all of the water at once. It made for slow walking. The water pushed against their boots harder, as if the current was picking up. It was still growing deeper as well. Soon there was no dry shoulder left.

"We have to go faster," he insisted, pulling on Tyler again. "The water is getting deeper fast. We have to find Max and get out of here."

By the time they reached the huge, columned area of the storm drains, the water had risen above their knees and quickly filled the rubber boots. "It's getting deeper," Tyler said. "We can't go that way any farther."

"We have to," Gabe insisted. "That's where Max was. We won't be able to get out without him."

Tyler pulled Gabe's arm. "We'll just have to find the spot where we came in. Or climb out somewhere else."

Gabe put his hands to his mouth and

bellowed. "Max! Mr. Payne! Where are you?" He listened for an answer but all he heard was the roar of rushing water. Tyler was right. They had to get out of there.

He looked around the wide storm drain. There were several spots where side drains emptied into the big room. Clearly, the one they'd been in wasn't the one that led back out, otherwise they would have crossed paths with Max Payne. So they needed to choose one of the other tunnel-like openings.

"Come on!" Tyler yelled again, trying to pull Gabe back into the drain.

Gabe shook his head. "We can't go back in this drain. It's not the right one. We have to go out through one of the others."

Tyler looked around. "Which one?"

Panic clawed at Gabe. Which one? He had no idea. He tried to remember which way they'd originally come. He wasn't sure. Still, there was

no choice. He had to pick a tunnel. He pointed. "That one."

"Okay, let's go."

Tyler and Gabe hung on to each other to keep the rushing water from sweeping them off their feet. The heavy boots made it hard to walk, but helped keep them from losing their footing. Still, they nearly fell several times, and grabbed at columns to avoid being swept away.

Finally they made it to the side drain. The water was shin high, and rising water from the ocean was pressing against the flow from the storm drains. Debris floated in the swirling water. Gabe was grateful that Tyler seemed to have forgotten the eel he had seen earlier. His focus, like Gabe's, was on pressing forward.

Up ahead, Gabe spotted rungs leading upwards. "There, we'll try that one."

They struggled towards it. Gabe knew it wasn't the way they'd come in, but all he wanted was to

get out. They'd deal with wherever they ended up. At least it would be dry and above ground. The rungs felt slightly slimy under Gabe's hands. When he reached the top, he pushed hard against the manhole. It didn't move at all. "It's stuck. Or maybe just too heavy. I can't move it."

Tyler crowded up the ladder beside him and together they shoved on the manhole cover. Again, there was no movement. "We need to climb higher," Tyler said. "If we can push with our backs and legs instead of our arms, we'll be stronger."

They climbed as high as they could, wedging themselves together, half doubled over with their backs against the manhole cover. They faced the swirling water below. They pushed using the strength of their legs on the rungs and their backs against the manhole. It didn't move at all.

"I think it might be sealed or something," Tyler said. "We need to try another one."

Gabe hated to climb back down into the water, but he had no idea how high it might reach. They climbed down and sloshed on. Now the water was thigh high and every step was a major struggle. The rubber boots were so heavy, that Gabe could do little more than shuffle, but he was afraid to kick them off. They were helping to keep them rooted to the ground.

They reached another set of railings and heaved themselves up them. Again, they struggled against the manhole cover but it wouldn't budge. "We should just wait here," Tyler said. "When the water goes back down, we can find the right way out."

"How do we know how high the water gets?" Gabe asked. "And how long does it take for the tide to turn? I don't know how long we can hold on."

Tyler laughed sadly. "I bet Sean could tell us exactly how long it is."

"I'm sure you're right," Gabe said. "But I also think it's hours and hours from now." He looked up at the manhole.

"We could call Ben," Tyler suggested. "He could come get us."

"How? By looking under every manhole in Queens? I don't know where we are."

Tyler looked down at the water. "We're going to die, aren't we?"

"Not if the water doesn't get too high." Gabe said, but already the water was lapping at their shoes. If it was hours and hours until it dropped, how much longer would it keep rising? Would it leave them any breathing room at all?

chapter 8
A NARROW ESCAPE

Tyler pressed against the manhole cover again. "Do you think it's been sealed shut? Or are we just too weak?"

"It doesn't much matter," Gabe answered. "We're just as stuck either way."

"Well, I was thinking maybe we should yell," Tyler said. "Then if someone heard us, they could open it from above and get us out."

Gabe didn't see how that could be a bad idea. So they both started screaming at the tops of their lungs. The sound echoed around them, bouncing back at them almost painfully. Still, they kept shouting until they had to stop and rest.

Then they heard splashing under them and it wasn't the normal splashing of the rising water.

"Someone's down here," Gabe said. He started yelling, but Tyler grabbed his shirt.

Tyler put his face close to Gabe's and spoke in a rough whisper. "What if it's not a person? What if it's an alligator? That Max guy said this would be the perfect place to find them. Maybe they swim up in the high tide and hunt."

"There aren't any alligators in the Atlantic around New York," Gabe said.

"Hey, all those news stories we saw, the alligators had to come from somewhere!"

"Yeah, pets and carnivals, places like that." Gabe yelled again for help, though Tyler kept shushing him.

"Stop it," Gabe snapped as Tyler tried to cover his mouth. "What if it's Max?"

The splashing grew louder and louder. Then a figure appeared under them. It wasn't Max. Instead, it was the homeless guy. "You guys aren't safe," he said urgently. "The water will reach

that manhole. Come down. We have to get out of here."

Gabe didn't need to be told twice. He scrambled down the ladder with Tyler right after him. The scruffy man was thin but tall, and surprisingly strong. The water was high on his waist which brought it high on Gabe's chest. The man kept hold of Gabe's arm with one hand and Tyler's with the other, and he just plowed along through the water.

The water kept rising as they walked. The man passed up one ladder. He just said, "Can't get out there." Gabe didn't argue with him. When he finally reached another ladder, the water was up to Gabe's chest and the pressure from it made it hard for Gabe to breathe. Things floated around them in the water, including something dead that Gabe thought might have been a rat.

The man hauled Tyler around to the ladder. "Up. Just go high enough to hold yourself out of the water!" Tyler didn't need any coaxing.

He scrambled up the ladder out of the water. Then it was Gabe's turn. When both boys were on the ladder, the man climbed up behind. "Can you boys give me room to pass?"

Tyler and Gabe swung to the side of the rungs, but the space was too tight for them to get far and the water still lapped at their waists. "Sorry," Gabe said.

The man looked up. "We'll have to all climb to the top."

They climbed together. It was tight, but the man freed one arm and pushed against the cover. It moved! Gabe and Tyler reached up to push too. In the tight confines, there was no way for them to fall so they didn't even bother holding onto the rungs. They reached up with both hands, shoving the heavy iron lid aside.

The manhole opened on a parking lot behind a fire station. As Gabe climbed out, he saw a group of fire fighters running out of the station

toward them. He knew they were in big trouble, but all he could be was grateful. He didn't doubt for a second that they would have drowned if the homeless man hadn't saved them.

The firemen helped haul Tyler and then the homeless man out of the manhole. "Dave," one of the fire fighters said. "What were you doing with kids down there? You know that storm sewer fills up."

"I was fishing," the homeless man said, "alone. But I heard yelling. It took a while to track down the sound, and I found these guys clinging to a ladder. I didn't take them down there."

"Dave?" Gabe asked.

The homeless man laughed. "Did you think homeless people don't have names?"

"I just didn't know what it was," Gabe mumbled. "You know these guys?"

"He used to be one of us guys," one of the firefighters said, clapping Dave on the back.

"You were a firefighter!" Tyler said, his eyes round as saucers.

"Everybody on the streets used to be someone else," Dave said. "I'd rather not talk about it." He turned to the firefighters. "Can you get these kids back where they belong? I need to get out of here. There are people waiting on this fish." Then he laughed and turned to Gabe. "You know, it was the conversation with your brother that reminded me about fishing for eels around here. So I guess that saved your life today."

Gabe hardly knew what to say. "I'm sure glad you had that talk then. Thanks for helping us."

"No problem." He turned to the firefighters again. "You'll get these kids home?"

"Sure, Dave," one of the men said. "Look, you know we're here for you, right?"

Dave nodded. "Thanks. Like I said, I need to go." He turned to Gabe and Tyler. "Stay out of the sewers."

"You definitely don't have to worry about that," Gabe told him.

The firefighters called Ben and then they let Gabe and Tyler use their showers. They also washed their clothes, loaning the boys T-shirts and sweat pants to wear while they waited.

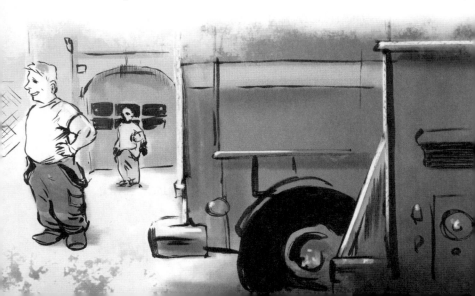

"Do you know why Dave is homeless?" Gabe asked one of the firefighters.

The man nodded. "He went into a building to save some people. Something fell on him and he almost died. We got Dave out, but no one could help the others. Dave couldn't get over it."

"Oh, wow," Gabe said.

"He sure saved us," Tyler said.

The firefighter laughed. "That's Dave. He does a lot of good for people even now. He's just not ready to be what he used to be."

"I don't know," Gabe said. "I think he's still what he used to be. He's a hero."

When Ben got there, Gabe braced himself for a lot of yelling. Instead, Ben rushed over and hugged Gabe. The yelling would come later, when Ben found out Max Payne had taken the boys into the sewer and abandoned them. The firefighters were mad about that too.

"At least you guys are okay," Ben said.

"I know it doesn't make up for what we did," Gabe said. "But we got some great footage in the sewers." He held up the camera. "I even got shots of something in the water."

"An alligator?" Ben said.

"An eel," Gabe said at the same moment that Tyler called out, "A snake!"

Gabe shrugged. "You'll see it. Anyway, you can use it for the show."

"You know the show isn't more important that your life," Ben said. "Why did you do something so stupid?"

"It sounded exciting," Gabe said weakly.

"He came because I was going to go without him," Tyler said. "It's not Gabe's fault. He just didn't want me going alone. I was the one who wasn't acting very smart. And I'm the one who ran off when I saw the snake. We'd have been fine except for that."

"Gabe had other choices besides going with

you," Ben insisted. "He could have called me, and I'd have put a stop to your adventure. At least this is the last investigation for the summer."

Gabe sighed. He looked down at his bare feet, nearly covered in the rolled-up pant legs of the borrowed sweat pants. "You'll probably hire an adult crew by next summer."

"Maybe," Ben said. "Though you guys will be older then."

"That's true," Gabe said hopefully.

"And smarter," Ben said.

"That's not a sure thing," Tyler admitted.

Ben shrugged. "I'm not looking for a sure thing. I like the mystery of finding out." He patted Tyler and Gabe on the back. "You're not out of trouble, but since we still have a last show to put together for this season, I guess we better stick together."

"That sounds like a plan to me," Gabe said, grinning.